TALES OF
Edgar Allan Poe

Retold Timeless Classics

Perfection Learning®

Retold by L. L. Owens

Editor: Susan Sexton
Illustrator: Michael A. Aspengren

For information, contact:
Perfection Learning® Corporation
Phone: 1-800-831-4190 • Fax: 1-712-644-2392
1000 North Second Avenue, P.O. Box 500
Logan, Iowa 51546-1099

Paperback ISBN 0-7891-2859-4
Cover Craft® ISBN 0-7807-7853-7
Printed in the U.S.A.
7 8 9 10 PP 08 07 06 05 04 03

Table of Contents

THE TELL-TALE HEART

It is true. I have been nervous lately. Very, very nervous!

Some say I am mad. Madness is considered a sickness. Isn't that what people think?

In any case, I am here to say this; I am anything but sick. In fact, I'm as healthy as can be. I can tell, because my senses are sharper than ever. Especially my sense of hearing.

Let me tell you the whole story. Then you can judge for yourself.

THE CRIME

I loved the old man. He'd been kind to me. Always. So I'm not sure where I got the idea.

But once I did, it haunted me day and night.

You see, he had this awful eye. The eye of a vulture. It was pale blue and cloudy. Whenever he looked at me, my blood ran cold. It seemed to stare at me every day.

Finally, I decided to get rid of it. That's right. I would kill the old man and rid myself of the eye forever.

You should have seen how cleverly I went about it. I left nothing to chance. Indeed, I was never nicer to the old man than during the days before I killed him.

At midnight, every night, I carefully turned the latch of his door. And I opened it—so gently! Then slowly, I put in a dark lantern—no light shone out. And then I stuck in my head.

You must understand that I needed to see the old man as he lay upon his bed. But I did not wish to disturb his sleep. Oh, you would laugh at how skillfully I moved my head in! I moved it slowly—so slowly. It often took an hour to ease my whole head through the opening.

You tell me. Would a madman have been so wise?

When my head was well into the room, I undid the lantern. Cautiously. I undid it just enough for a single ray to stream out. And I aimed the beam directly at the horrible eye.

I did this seven nights in a row. Precisely at midnight. But the eye was always closed.

This made it impossible for me to do my work. Remember, it was not the old man who vexed me. It was his Evil Eye.

Each morning at daybreak, I went boldly into his chamber. I greeted him with a hearty "Good morning!" And I asked how he'd slept.

He had no reason to suspect that I knew the answer.

On the eighth night, it took an unusually long time to open the door. The minute hand on a watch moves more quickly than my own hand did.

I was alive with the thrill of my own power. To think that I was there, opening the door, little by little. And he did not even dream of my plot! I think I may have chuckled at the idea. For he moved suddenly, as if startled.

Now you probably think that I drew back at this. But I did not. His room was pitch-black. So I knew that he could not see the door's opening. I kept pushing it forward. Steadily. Silently.

My head was in at last. I was about to open the lantern. But my thumb slipped and rattled the tin fastening.

The old man sprang up in bed. He cried, "Who's there?"

I kept quite still. I said nothing. For an hour, I stayed frozen.

In the meantime, I did not hear him lay down. He sat up, listening.

Presently, he groaned. I knew it was the groan of mortal terror. I knew the sound well. I pitied the old man. Yet I smiled. For I guessed that he'd been laying awake since he'd first stirred in the bed. His fears had been growing ever since.

He had no doubt been trying to comfort himself. I could imagine him thinking, "It's just the wind in the chimney." Or, "Perhaps a mouse is crossing the floor."

The shadow of Death, however, had wrapped itself around him. He neither saw nor heard the presence of my head. But he felt it.

At length, I resolved to uncover a tiny crack in the lantern. I opened it, ever so slightly. A single, dim ray—like a spider's thread—shot out from the crack. And it lit up the vulture eye.

The eye was wide open. I grew furious as I gazed upon it. I saw it clearly. It was a murky blue that chilled my very bones. I could see nothing else. For I had directed the ray, as if by instinct, precisely upon the cursed spot.

Have I mentioned my keen senses? They are extraordinary, I assure you. What happened next will prove it.

To my ears came a low, dull, quick sound. Like that of a watch wrapped in cotton. No—it was the sound of the old man's heartbeat. This increased my fury tenfold.

Even so, I kept still. I scarcely breathed. I held the lantern motionless. One might well be surprised at how steadily I fixed the ray upon the eye.

Meanwhile, the drumming of the heart continued. It grew quicker and louder with every passing second.

The old man's terror must have been extreme! But what about mine? I've already admitted that I am nervous. And so I was then.

It was the dead of night, after all. And the dark silence of that old house only increased the pulsing noise. It drove me into an uncontrollable terror. Yet I stood still as the beating of his heart grew louder, stronger!

His heart will surely burst! I thought. I must stop that awful pounding. Or a neighbor will hear.

And so the old man's time had come. With a yell, I lunged at him. He shrieked once—and once only. In a flash, I dragged him to the floor. And I pulled the heavy bed over him.

I smiled merrily. The deed was done! But for many minutes, that heart beat on. The sound was muffled, to be sure. But it was still there. This did not trouble me. For no one else could possibly hear it. And after a while, it stopped.

I moved the bed and took a look. I checked for a pulse. There was none. He was dead, all right. Stone dead. His eye would plague me no more.

THE COVER-UP

Do you still think I am mad? You won't for long. Not after I describe how I hid the body.

The night was dwindling away. So I hurried. First, I cut up the corpse. I cut off the head. Then the arms. And, finally, the legs.

I pulled up three planks from the flooring. And deposited the body parts underneath. I replaced the boards perfectly. No human eye could have detected the slightest change.

Best of all, there was nothing to clean up. No stain of any kind! I had artfully let a tub catch all the blood!

It was still dark when I finished. As the clock struck four, I heard a firm knock at the street door. I opened it with a light heart. For what did I have to fear?

Three men stood in the entrance. "We are officers of the police," they said.

"Welcome. Do come in," said I.

"A neighbor reported hearing a shriek," explained one.

"We are here to search the premises," added another.

"Ah," I smiled. For what had I to fear? "The shriek was my own. I was dreaming. And something startled me."

I went on to say that the old man was visiting friends in the country. Then I took my visitors all over the house.

"Please search," I said. "Search well!"

Soon, I led them to the old man's bedroom. I felt elated. For they knew nothing! I showed them his treasures. Everything was in its place. Then I excused myself for a moment. And I reappeared with some chairs.

You probably find that odd. But the thrill of my secret was ruling my actions. I felt perfectly safe.

"Why don't you good men sit down for a moment," I offered.

They were happy to do so. I placed my own seat over the very spot beneath which the victim lay. It was a bold—yet delicious—move on my part.

The officers had believed me! My easy manner had convinced them. So we all sat and chatted for a while. Before long, however, I became impatient. Oh, how I wished them gone!

My head ached. And there was a persistent ringing in my ears. It was dreadful! But still they sat. And still they chatted.

The ringing continued. It became louder and clearer. Finally, I realized that the noise was not within my ears. There is no doubt that I grew very pale.

I began talking more energetically. And in a louder voice. But I could not cover up the sound. It had become a low, dull, quick sound. The sound of a watch wrapped in cotton.

I gasped. Still the officers did not hear it.

Again, I talked louder. But the noise only increased.

I got up and babbled about unimportant matters. I used a shrill tone and wild gestures. Still, the noise increased.

Will these men never leave? I agonized.

As a signal that our chat was over, I paced the floor. But the officers stayed. And the noise steadily increased.

I could stand it no longer!

THE TRUTH

I foamed. And I raved. I swung my chair and beat it upon the boards. But the noise was stronger. It grew louder—louder—louder! And yet the men continued to chat and smile.

Was it possible they did not hear this noise? No! I was certain that they heard it! They knew! And they were mocking my horror! Anything was better than the scorn they showed me! I could bear their smirks no longer! I knew that I must scream now or die! And still—listen! The noise grew louder! louder! louder! louder!

"Cads!" I shrieked. "Stop this degrading show! I admit it! I killed him! Tear up the planks! Right here! You hear the sound! It is the beating of his hideous heart!"

The Oval Portrait

I took a great fall from my horse while traveling through the country. I hit my head. And I was in need of rest. So my valet and I broke into an abandoned manor. We planned to stay just for the night.

We settled ourselves in one of the smallest apartments. It was in a remote tower of the building.

The tower's decorations were tattered and old. Tapestries hung on the walls. And so did a number of very lively paintings.

I had my valet light the candles. He placed them at the head of the bed. In case I couldn't sleep, I thought, I could look at these pictures. And I could read the booklet near the bedside that described them.

I read and gazed at the paintings for a long, long time. The hours flew by. Until, that is, the deep midnight came. Suddenly, the angle of the light was all wrong. I adjusted the candles. But their new positions did little to brighten my reading spot.

Instead, the light fell upon what had been a dark corner. And I noticed another painting.

Before me was the portrait of a young woman. I glanced at it quickly, then closed my eyes. Why I did this was not obvious to me at first.

My vision has tricked me, I thought.

After a few seconds, I looked again. The fog in my head—present since my fall—had lifted. And I was fully alert.

As I said, the portrait was of a young woman. Head and shoulders only. The rest of her melted into the deep shadows of the painting's background. The oval frame was richly gilded.

Indeed, it was a beautiful work of art. But

that in itself could not have affected me so deeply.

What had moved me so?

I'll tell you. The woman's head had looked real. Like there was a living person right there on the canvas!

I stared at the oval portrait for another hour.

After much thought, I became satisfied. I'd finally found the key to the painting's power. It was simple, really.

You see, the artist had created a perfectly lifelike expression. *Anyone* looking at the image for the first time would find it startling.

I was relieved. And I became eager to settle in for some sleep. I was about to snuff out the candles when a thought occurred to me.

I'll just read about the portrait first. It won't take a moment. Then I'll slumber.

Turning to the correct page, I read the strange words that follow.

She was a maiden of rarest beauty. And she was full of glee. Evil was the hour when she married the painter. He, you see, already had a bride—his Art.

She was lovely and full of life. She cherished all things. All things, that is, except her husband's Art. It was her rival. And she hated it! For it deprived her of his love.

When the painter asked his young bride to sit for him, she shuddered. But she was by nature a humble and giving woman. So she agreed to do it.

She sat quietly for many weeks in the tower-chamber. Sometimes, the only light in the room came from the chandelier overhead.

The painter reveled in his work. It went on hour after hour. And day after day. He became one with his brush.

Meanwhile, the gloom of the tower claimed the soul of his bride. She grew weaker with every day.

Yet she smiled steadily. On and on. And she never complained.

After all, she reasoned. He is working day and night to depict *me!*

Visitors who saw the portrait were overwhelmed. They spoke in hushed tones of the resemblance. And of the deep love the painter must feel for his subject.

As the portrait neared completion, the artist barred visitors from the tower.

The painter had gone insane with the zeal for his work!

He rarely turned away from the canvas. Not even to look at his wife. So he never saw the obvious. That the colors he brushed upon the canvas were draining from his bride's cheeks.

Many weeks passed. The painter had little left to do. One stroke here to finish the mouth. Another stroke there to tint the eye.

This done, the young woman's spirit rose up for a moment. It sputtered and flickered like an ember.

The painter set down his brush. His work was complete. For a moment, he gazed at it, spellbound. But then his face grew pale. And he began to tremble.

Breathlessly, he cried, "This is Life itself!" Then he whirled around to look at his beloved wife.

She was dead!

Morella

I was so fond of my friend Morella. We met by accident many years ago. I took an instant—and very intense—liking to her.

I say "liking" because I want to make it clear. I had great affection for her—even love. But the love was not romantic. It was respectful, though. And impossible to ignore.

Fate stepped in. And Morella and I married. Happily, yes!

Morella's intelligence was gigantic. In many ways, I was her pupil. She loved to have me read mystical German writings. These were her pets. And she studied them constantly.

I grew to love them too. Morella's influence saw to it. In time, we talked of nothing but these books.

◈ ◈ ◈

Seasons changed. And my wife's manner began to disturb me. I could no longer bear her touch. The sound of her voice sent shudders up my spine. And a look from her lifeless eyes was enough to make me ill.

She knew all this, naturally. But she accepted it, smiling. She even called it our destiny.

One day, a large red spot appeared on her cheek. The veins on her pale forehead were pulsing and blue. I pitied her at first.

But then I met her glance. In the next instant, I became fairly giddy. May I say that I became consumed with a single desire? A desire for the moment of Morella's death?

Morella clung to life for many weeks. Then the months wore on. My nerves were tortured. And I grew furious at the delay.

Like a fiend, I cursed the bitter moments of her life. Moments that seemed only to lengthen as Morella's life slipped away.

One fall evening, Morella called me to her bedside.

"I am dying," she declared softly.

I kissed her forehead. And she continued.

"I am dying. Yet I shall live."

"Morella!"

"You were never able to love me. Not in life," she said coldly. "But in my death, you shall adore me."

"Morella!"

"I repeat—I am dying. But I am about to give you a child," Morella revealed. "When my spirit leaves, the child shall appear. It is our child. Yours and mine. Your days shall be days of sorrow. For the hours of your happiness are gone. And joy does not come twice in a life."

"Morella!" I cried. "Morella! A child? Why didn't you tell me?"

But she turned away. She gasped as our child was born. Then she fell limp. She was dead. And I heard her voice no more.

The child—a daughter—took her first breath as her mother took her last. She grew into the perfect image of Morella. And I loved her with all my heart.

The child grew strangely. Quickly. But stranger still was the rapid development of her mind. This child was wise and cunning and mature!

I hid her from the world. Destiny had forced me to adore her. And I could not bear to share her.

The years rolled away. And the child became identical to her mother. In every way. Her smile was like her mother's. It made me shiver.

Her eyes were like Morella's too. Sometimes they stared into mine, sending me Morella's own powerful message.

Her high forehead and silky ringlets were Morella's. And her thin fingers—even the tone of her voice—began to fill me with terror.

When my daughter was ten, I realized that I had never named her. "My child," I'd always said. Or, "My love."

Morella's name had died with her. I had never spoken of Morella to the child. It would have been impossible.

But I knew that the girl needed a name. "You shall be baptized tomorrow," I announced to her.

During the ceremony, the time came for me to declare a name. But I paused. There were so many beautiful ones to choose from. There were old and modern names. And there were favorites that were gentle, happy, and good.

I do not know what demon urged me to say what I did. But I whispered "Morella" in the holy man's ear.

When the preacher said the name, my child flailed wildly about. She turned her glassy eyes upward. And she fell upon the black slabs of our family vault.

"I am here!" she cried.

I heard those few simple sounds. And I tried to comprehend them. Years may pass, but I will never forget that moment. Or what happened next.

I went into a dreamlike state. All I could see was Morella. All I could hear was "Morella!"

She died. And I carried her to the tomb with my own hands.

I opened the vault to lay the second Morella next to the first. And then I laughed. A long and bitter laugh. For I found no traces of the first Morella!

The Cask of Amontillado

Fortunato had insulted me. So I vowed revenge. Not in so many words, of course. Never aloud.

So Fortunato had no reason to think that I meant him harm. I continued to smile whenever we met. He had no idea that I was smiling at the thought of his death.

I had given quite a bit of thought to finding Fortunato's weakness. It was hard. For he was well respected. And many feared him.

Then it hit me. Fortunato fancied himself a wine expert.

"That's it!" I cried. I was so delighted with my own genius. I fairly danced about my house! "It won't be long now!" I promised myself.

I planned a "chance meeting" with Fortunato. It was Carnival time. And I knew he would celebrate.

An Unsuspecting Fool

Saturday evening came. I dismissed my servants for the rest of the weekend. "Go!" I told them. "Have a good time at Carnival!"

When I found Fortunato, he wore a jester's costume. He was slightly tipsy from the wine he'd drunk at the festival.

"Hello there, good man!" he exclaimed. He was certainly glad to see me. There were bells on his pointed cap. And they jingled merrily as he shook my hand.

"Ah, Fortunato! Hello!" I acted surprised. "How lucky for me. I need some of your expert advice."

"How can I help, my friend?" he asked.

"I just bought a cask of Amontillado," I began. Then I paused to see whether I had his attention. I did. This subject was dear to him.

"Amontillado?" he urged. "Go on."

So I continued. "Yes, Amontillado. I paid a nice price indeed. Now I fear that I have been tricked. It does not taste like Amontillado to me. At least not exactly. That's why I need your help. Someone with your knowledge can confirm my suspicions. Or you can make them go away."

"I'll have to see for myself," Fortunato declared. "I doubt that anyone would have genuine Amontillado right now. Not during Carnival. Where are you keeping it?"

"It's at home. In my vaults," I replied.

"Let us go then."

"That is very kind of you," I said. "But it is late. And you were on your way home. The wine will be there tomorrow. Besides, you are not dressed properly. It is cold, and the vaults are very damp. You'll be most uncomfortable."

"Nonsense," he insisted. "The cold is of no consequence to me. Come! I want to taste that Amontillado!"

Fortunato took my arm and turned us toward my estate. As we walked, I kept my cloak tightly closed. And I put on a black silk mask. "For the cold," I said to my good friend Fortunato.

Into the Darkness

Once home, I offered Fortunato a torch. Then I led him down a long, winding staircase.

"Do be careful," I said.

"Don't worry about me," he replied. The bells on his cap jangled with each step.

Finally, we reached the bottom. We had entered my family's catacombs. All the Montresors are buried there.

Fortunato looked around. "Where is the cask?" he asked.

"This way," I said. "Follow me."

Then he began to cough. He choked and sputtered for several moments. When he caught his breath, I said, "Let's turn back. The dampness down here is making you ill."

"Don't be ridiculous!" he replied. "I'm perfectly well. A bit of a cough won't kill me."

"You're right. A cough won't kill you. Here, let me get you a drink." I pointed to a long rack of wine bottles. "A drop of this Medoc will warm us up. It will stave off your sickness too."

I reached for a bottle and broke off its neck against the wall.

"Drink this," I said.

He took the bottle from my outstretched hand. Before sipping from it, he toasted, "To the dead that rest around us."

"Here, here! To your long life," I replied. And I motioned for him to follow me.

As we walked, he remarked, "These vaults are very large."

"True. We Montresors were a great family."

"Tell me—what is your coat of arms?"

"A golden foot on a blue background. The foot is crushing a serpent."

"And your motto?"

"No one insults me without punishment," I replied.

"A good one!" he said. The wine showed in his eyes. "And now, on to the Amontillado!"

"On to the Amontillado!" I agreed.

We continued our journey. We passed through generations of piled bones. And under a series of low arches. Then we descended more stairs—two sets—until we arrived at a deep crypt. Three of its walls had been lined with human remains. They were piled high—all the way up to the vault overhead.

The fourth wall had not been finished. Or some of it had been knocked down. It is hard to say.

"Here we are," I said cheerily. "The

Amontillado is on the other side of this wall. It's in a special cask."

Fortunato held his torch high. The flame was rather low in the dense air. So it was difficult for him to see what lay ahead.

"Why did you choose to store it here?" he asked.

The space was about three feet wide, four feet deep, and six feet high. It was backed by a wall of solid rock.

"Go on in," I urged. "Amontillado—straight ahead!"

He stepped over the low wall and into the small area. I followed on his heels. He reached the end of the space at once. He stood still for a moment, confused by the whole situation.

In the blink of an eye, I had chained him to the wall!

A Cruel Fate

You see, there were two large iron staples in the rock. They were about two feet apart. From one staple hung a short chain. From the other hung a padlock. I worked swiftly. Fortunato was too stunned to resist.

Once I'd locked him up, I stepped back over the wall.

"I offered to let you turn around," I said, shrugging. "Let me offer again. What's that? No? Then I shall be forced to leave you."

"But—but—the Amontillado!" cried my friend. "Montresor—the Amontillado!" He was still in shock.

"Indeed!" I said. "The Amontillado!"

With that, I produced a trowel from under my cloak. Then I found my stash of supplies—building stone, mortar, and so on. Hastily, I began to wall up the entrance to the space.

I soon realized that the effects of the wine Fortunato had drunk had worn off. He moaned, "I do not understand. I do not understand."

Then he grew silent. This lasted for quite some time.

I worked hard. Soon, I had laid the third row, then the fourth.

Fortunato tried to break free. He shook his chains mightily for several minutes. I wanted to enjoy the spectacle. So I stopped my work and sat down upon the bones for a bit.

My dear friend tired and quieted himself. And I resumed my work. I completed the next three rows—up to my chest—with vigor. Again, I paused. I stuck my torch over the wall to have a look.

Suddenly, Fortunato let loose with several

loud, forceful, mad screams. I took a step back. I even trembled.

But then I realized that Fortunato could do me no harm. Not from his position! So I went back to work. I matched his screams in volume and strength until he grew still.

The Last Stone

Midnight—and my task was nearly complete. I had finished three more rows. There was just one more to go.

I fitted the final stone. As I prepared to plaster it, a low laugh rose up from behind the fresh wall. The hairs on the back of my neck stood up at the sound of it.

The sad voice that called out baffled me. Surely, this cannot be the voice of the strong, noble Fortunato. The voice said—

"Ha! ha! ha! Hee! hee! hee! What a very good joke indeed. An excellent jest, Montresor. We'll laugh about this later. Ho! ho! ho! Oh, yes. We will enjoy this story for years to come. We can tell it to our wives over some wine."

"Perhaps some Amontillado!" I taunted.

"Ho! ho! ho! Yes, of course! Amontillado! But now, we must hurry. Will they not be waiting for us—the Lady Fortunato and the rest? Come now. Let us be gone."

"Yes," I said. "Let us be gone!"

"For the love of God, Montresor!"

"Yes," I said. "For the love of God!"

This time, Fortunato did not reply. I grew restless. I called out. "Fortunato!"

Still, nothing. Again I called. "Fortunato!"

I thrust my torch through the small hole that remained. I let it drop. A jingling of the jester's bells was the only response.

My heart grew sick. The dampness of the catacombs was getting to me.

With renewed energy, I forced the last stone into place. I plastered it up. The mortar would dry in time. Then I piled my ancestral bones high in front of the new wall. And for half of a century, no mortal has disturbed them.

May he rest in peace!

Annabel Lee

Long ago, in a kingdom by the sea, lived
*   a beautiful maiden.*
Her name was Annabel Lee.
This maiden wanted one thing. And one
*   thing only—*
To share her love with me.
We were young. And love was new.
Yet that love was deep. And pure. And
*   true.*

Annabel Lee's father disapproved. He warned his daughter to stay away from me.

"You are merely a child," he said to his daughter. "You know nothing of love. Soon, you will forget him."

"Oh, Father, no! Never!" she cried. "He is my love!"

"I am sorry, my dear. He is not of our station. So I cannot let you see him. It is for the best."

Annabel Lee burst into tears. Her father stroked her hair. "There, there," he said gently.

"Please don't cry. One day, you will thank me. Just wait and see."

Annabel Lee was allowed to see me one last time. We were supposed to say good-bye. Instead, we made a pact.

"We shall run away together," we vowed. "Tomorrow, just before dawn." It was the only way.

We came together on a rocky shore. And I lifted her onto my horse.

"It is still early," I said. "We can ride for hours before we are missed."

But, alas, it was not to be. Two of her father's men had followed Annabel Lee. They rode toward us on their horses.

"Young lady!" called one of the men. "You will come with us. Your father is waiting." He snatched Annabel Lee from my horse. She screamed wildly.

"Let her go!" I roared. "In the name of the angels in heaven!"

But the angels did not help us that day. Not even they could grasp the truth of our devotion.

The other man held me back until they were gone. When he let me go, I lunged at him. But he knocked me down with a swift kick to my jaw.

I never saw my beloved again. I tried. But

her father had locked her up in a secret tower. I heard that she died there—of a broken heart—as the cold wind blew across the sea.

Many years have come and gone. But I have never forgotten my precious Annabel Lee. I am told that she is here—resting forever—in the depths of the uncaring sea.

Now, as I walk along the fateful shores, the clouds part. And a ray of sunshine lights the spot where I lost my heart. This, I'm sure, is a sign from above. The angels have learned the meaning of true love.

As for the two of us, our love lives on. Time and space are meaningless. Our souls, forever one.

For the moon never beams without bringing me dreams—
Of the beautiful Annabel Lee.
And the stars never rise, but I feel the bright eyes—
Of the beautiful Annabel Lee.
And so, all the night-tide, I lie down by the side—
Of my darling—my darling—my life and my bride—
In her tomb 'neath the cold, thrashing sea.

SOME WORDS WITH A MUMMY

I had an awful headache. And I was very sleepy. So I ate my supper quickly.

I had a light supper, of course. Welsh rabbit. I know it is unwise to eat more than a pound of it sometimes. Still, there can be no real objection to two pounds. And really, what is the difference between two and three pounds? It is only one pound!

My best guess is that I ate four pounds of Welsh rabbit that night. My wife would say it was five. But she is confused. Five is the number of Brown Stouts I drank with it.

In any case, I finished my meal. And I climbed into bed. I fell instantly into a happy sleep.

Later, I awoke to the sound of my doorbell. Then someone was knocking—even pounding—at the street door. While I was still rubbing my eyes, my wife thrust a note in my face. It was from my old friend, Doctor Ponnonner. It said:

Come to my house at once. I have permission from the City Museum to examine the Mummy. You know the one I mean! Just a few friends will be here. We shall unroll the Mummy at 11.

Yours,

Ponnonner

I leaped out of bed and got dressed. In no time, I arrived at the doctor's house. The others were already there. The Mummy was on the dining table. The moment I got there, the examination began.

The Mummy had been discovered by Captain Arthur Sabretash (Ponnonner's cousin). The tomb had been in the mountains—above Thebes on the Nile.

For eight years, the coffin had been on display at the museum. But now, *we* had the coffin—and the body inside.

The case was about seven feet long. It was three feet wide and two-and-a-half feet deep. It was oblong—not coffin-shaped.

It was made out of papier-mâché. And it was richly decorated with funeral scenes. There were *hieroglyphics,* or characters, on it. Luckily, Mr. Gliddon was in our party. He could read the characters and tell us what they said.

It was hard to get the case open. But once we did, we found a smaller coffin-shaped case inside. It was a perfect copy of the first.

We opened it. There was a third case. It was the same as the first two. Except that it was made of cedar. The Mummy's body was in this one.

We had expected to find the Mummy wrapped up. Probably in linen bandages. Instead, it wore a papyrus covering. And the covering was coated with a layer of plaster. On it were many pictures.

The pictures showed many human and godlike forms. And there were hieroglyphics from head to foot.

Colorful glass beads hung around the Mummy's neck. There were also beads around his waist.

We stripped off the covering. The body's reddish flesh was in excellent condition.

There was no odor. And the skin was hard, smooth, and glossy.

The teeth and hair also looked good. And it looked as if beautiful glass balls replaced the eyes. The fingers and the nails had been painted with gold.

Mr. Gliddon noted, "The Mummy is embalmed." Then he sniffed the air and added, "Probably with camphor and other sweet-scented gums."

We searched the body very carefully. We were looking for openings through which the entrails, or guts, had been removed. But we found none!

So Doctor Ponnonner prepared his instruments. He was going to dissect the Mummy.

I spoke up. For it was past two o'clock. We agreed to hold off the internal exam.

"We'll meet tomorrow evening," we said.

We would have left at that point. If, that is, Gliddon hadn't made a suggestion.

"Why don't we try an experiment with the batteries," he said. "Just for sport."

Now the idea of applying electricity to a 4,000-year-old mummy was interesting. We loved it. So, mostly in jest, we set up a battery in the doctor's study.

Then we struggled to cut back some of the Mummy's skin. It was difficult. Finally, we attached the wires to his skull.

When nothing happened, we had a good laugh at ourselves. But suddenly, I caught a glimpse of something quite amazing.

"The Mummy's eyes!" I shouted. "The eyelids are fluttering!"

I can hardly describe the depths of our fright.

But we did calm down. Eventually. And we decided to hold further tests.

We readjusted the battery. Then we exposed a toe muscle and attached the wire.

With a sudden jerk, the Mummy drew up his right knee. He kicked Doctor Ponnonner—hard! The doctor shot through a window and to the street below.

We rushed out to help him. He met us on the staircase. He was up and ready to try again. Much to our surprise, he did just that.

The effect was electric, indeed!

First, the Mummy's eyes blinked quickly for several minutes. Second, the Mummy sneezed. Third, it sat up. Fourth, it shook its fist in Doctor Ponnonner's face. And fifth, it addressed Gliddon and Buckingham in Egyptian.

"Gentlemen!" he exclaimed. "I am shocked at your behavior. Doctor Ponnonner is a fool. He knows no better. So I pity him.

"But you, Mr. Gliddon! And Buckingham—you've lived in Egypt. You speak Egyptian as well as your own language. You have always been regarded as a friend to the mummies. I expected more of you!"

He continued, wildly. "What am I to think? You permit Tom, Dick, and Harry to strip me of my coffins—and my clothes! It's cold in here!"

You're no doubt wondering how we all responded. One might assume that we became hysterical. Or that we ran. Or simply fainted. But we didn't. Oddly, none of us acted as though anything unusual had just happened.

For my part, I merely stepped aside. I wanted to stay clear of the Egyptian's fist!

Doctor Ponnonner thrust his hands into his pockets. Then he glared at the Mummy and grew red in the face. Mr. Gliddon stroked his whiskers. And Mr. Buckingham hung his head.

The Mummy said with a sneer, "Why don't you speak, Mr. Buckingham? Didn't you hear what I said?"

Mr. Buckingham shuffled nervously from foot to foot. But he didn't answer.

The Mummy turned to Mr. Gliddon. He demanded to know what was going on.

Mr. Gliddon explained in Egyptian.

(Let me note something here. The rest of the conversations involving the Mummy were carried out in Egyptian. Gliddon and Buckingham interpreted for the rest of us.)

Mr. Gliddon tried to explain our motives to the Mummy. He spoke of the scientific benefits of studying mummies. Then he offered an apology for any trouble we had caused him.

The Mummy accepted the explanation and our apologies. Then he got down from the table. And he shook hands all around.

That done, we set about repairing the damage we'd done. We stitched up the gash on the Mummy's forehead. We bandaged his foot. And we applied a square inch of black plaster to his nose.

The doctor hastily fetched some clothes from his chamber. He returned with the following items.

a black dress coat
a pair of sky-blue plaid pants with straps
a pink gingham shirt
a patterned silk vest

a white-sack overcoat
a walking cane with a hook
a hat with no brim
patent-leather boots
straw-colored kid gloves
an eyeglass
a scarf

The Egyptian was about half the doctor's size. So we just sort of hung the clothes on him. One might have even been able to say that he was dressed!

Mr. Gliddon led him to a comfortable chair. The doctor rang for the servants. And he ordered refreshments by the fire.

The talk soon turned lively. We were so very curious.

"Tell me something," said Mr. Buckingham. "Isn't it high time you were dead?"

"Why, no!" replied the Mummy, astonished. "I am little more than 700 years old. My father lived to be 1,000."

A brisk series of calculations followed. It became clear to us that the Captain had misjudged the Mummy's age. It had been at least 5,050 years since he had been placed in his tomb!

Mr. Buckingham explained our discussion to the Mummy. "You said that you were 700. But

I was not referring to your age at the time you entered the tomb. I was wondering when you were placed there. I think we figured it out."

"Yes," nodded the Mummy. "I think I understand what you mean."

"Well, now *we* do not understand something," said Doctor Ponnonner. "You died and were buried in Egypt 5,000 years ago. So how are you here today? You know—alive. And looking so well?"

"Ah, but I was not, as you say, *dead,*" replied the Mummy. "I had fallen into a coma. And my friends decided that I was either dead or should be. So they embalmed me at once. I guess that you know about our embalming process?"

"Not altogether."

"What a sad state of ignorance you live in! Very well. I won't give all the details. Briefly, if the person was dead when he was embalmed, then he is dead now. But if he was alive at that time, he is alive today. I, for example, was embalmed alive. And that is why you can see me now."

"Then," said the doctor, "there may be other *live* mummies?"

"There is no question," replied the Mummy. "Many people from my tribe were embalmed alive. Some were embalmed by accident. Others were embalmed on purpose. All of them still remain in the tomb."

"Will you kindly explain that?" I asked. "What do you mean by *embalmed on purpose?*"

"Well," began the Mummy, "the normal span of a man's life was about 800 years. In my time, few men died before the age of 600. And few lived longer than 1,000 years.

"One day, embalming was discovered. And our philosophers had an idea. They wanted to divide this natural life term into parts."

The Mummy noticed our puzzled stares. "Let me explain the *parts,*" he offered. "A man might live for 200 years. He would get embalmed and rest for 1,000 years. Then he would be revived and live for 500 years. And so on."

We all nodded as if we understood. But how could we? The Egyptian went on.

"If we could do this," he said, "we could learn so much. The field of science could advance. And history, indeed, would become clearer."

"Forgive me, sir," interrupted Mr. Gliddon. "But I'm afraid you've lost me."

Gliddon was right. We were all lost in a stupor of new information.

So the Mummy continued. "Consider this. A historian, having lived to be 500, would write a book. Then he would get himself carefully embalmed. He would leave instructions to be revived in 600 years.

"At this time, he would no doubt find many different opinions about what his book meant. He would thus rewrite it. So the current generation of people could understand it.

"*Then* he would find out what else the moderns were saying about his time period. He would be able to correct whatever misinformation there was. This process has kept Egyptian history alive. And accurate!"

As you can guess, this set off another flurry of questions. We begged the Mummy to share his knowledge.

I asked, "What about astrology?" And my friends had questions of their own.

"What are your thoughts on democracy?"

"Tell us about your religious traditions."

The Mummy addressed each question in great detail. It was clear that modern man was no match for his clever people.

At one point, Dr. Ponnonner became excited. He exclaimed, "But look at *our* architecture!" (He had been feeling envious of

Egyptian knowledge. And he thought he'd found the perfect example of modern superiority.)

"For example," he said, "the Bowling Green Fountain in New York! Or the Capitol at Washington, D.C.!"

The doctor then described the Capitol. He said that the entrance alone had no less than 420 columns. The columns were five feet in diameter and ten feet apart.

"Hmmm," replied the Mummy. "I wish I could remember exactly. But there was one *small* palace I knew in Carnac. It had 144 columns. They were 37 feet around. And 25 feet apart."

The Mummy continued. "To get there from the Nile, one had to travel a two-mile avenue. It had sphinxes, statues, and pillars— 20, 60, and 100 feet tall!" He paused for effect.

"Now the palace itself was two miles long. And I think it was seven miles in circuit. Its walls were richly painted—inside and out— with hieroglyphics.

"Why, I'd say that 200 of your Capitols might have been squeezed into that palace. With a little effort, of course!"

He added, "You're right about one thing,

Doctor Ponnonner. I cannot ignore it. The Fountain at the Bowling Green is magnificent. Superior. Nothing like it has ever been seen in Egypt—or anywhere else!"

The doctor was shattered. He just shook his head. Then a light seemed to go on in his mind. "Tell me, sir," the doctor said gleefully. "Wouldn't the people of Egypt be impressed by the cleverness of modern dress?"

The Egyptian glanced at his pantaloons. Then he examined the end of one of his coat-tails. Slowly, his mouth turned up from ear to ear. But I don't recall that he spoke.

Our moods lightened. And the doctor approached the Mummy with great dignity.

"May I ask one more thing—upon your honor as a gentleman?"

"Of course."

"Have the Egyptians heard of, at any time, the manufacture of Ponnonner's lozenges? Or Brandreth's pills?"

The Egyptian blushed and hung his head. He had no answer! Clearly, the doctor had finally bested the Mummy.

The sight of the poor Mummy's embarrassment was great. He was unable to overcome his shame. Soon, his shame turned to anger.

I could not bear to watch it. So I grabbed my hat, bowed to him stiffly, and left.

It was past four o'clock in the morning when I got home. And I went to bed immediately.

It is now 10:23 A.M. I have been up since seven. I've been writing these notes for the benefit of my family. And, of course, for mankind.

I will not see my family again. My wife is a shrew. So I will not miss her.

The truth is, I am heartily sick of this life. I'm sick of the 19th century in general. Everything is falling apart. Besides, I am eager to know who will be president in 2045. Or if there will even be one!

I'm off to shave. And to swallow a quick cup of coffee. Then I will walk over to Ponnonner's. I've decided to get embalmed for a couple hundred years.

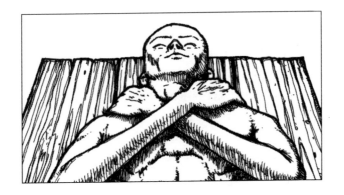

SOME WORDS
WITH A MUMMY

The Play

Cast of Characters

Narrator

John's Wife

John

Doctor Ponnonner

Mr. Gliddon

Mr. Buckingham

The Mummy

Setting: Boston in 1850

<u>Act I</u>

Narrator: John had an awful headache. And he was very sleepy. So he ate his supper quickly. He ate Welsh rabbit. He knew it was a mistake to eat more than a pound of it at once. But he loved it so much that he ate four pounds that night. His wife was angry when she saw how much he'd eaten.

John's Wife: You ate all that Welsh rabbit tonight! Now we don't have any leftovers. How could you?

Narrator: John ignored his wife and finished his meal. Then he climbed into bed. He fell right to sleep. Later, the doorbell woke him. Then someone knocked—even pounded—at the street door. While John was still rubbing his eyes, his wife thrust a note in his face. It was from his old friend, Doctor Ponnonner. It said:

> *Come to my house at once. I have permission from the City Museum to examine the Mummy. You know the one I mean! Just a few friends will be here. We shall unroll the Mummy at 11.*
>
> *Yours,*
> *Ponnonner*

John leaped out of bed and dressed.

John's Wife: Where are you going? It's late! I thought you were tired.

John: Never you mind. Don't wait up. I may be a while.

John's Wife: Take your time. I could use a break from your snoring.

Act II

Narrator: John raced to the doctor's house. His friends were already there. The Mummy was on the dining table.

Doctor Ponnonner: Let the examination begin!

Narrator: For eight years, the coffin had been on display at the museum. But now these men had the coffin—and the body inside.

The coffin was made out of papier-mâché. And it was richly decorated with funeral scenes. There were hieroglyphics on it too.

Mr. Gliddon: Those characters give important information. These right here represent the name of the dead.

Doctor Ponnonner: Do tell us what it says.

Mr. Gliddon: His name was Allamistakeo. He was quite wealthy. And he was an important member of his tribe.

Narrator: The men opened the case. They found a smaller coffin-shaped case inside. It was a perfect copy of the first. Then there was a third case—the same as the first two. But it was made of cedar. The Mummy's body was inside.

Mr. Buckingham: Look at that! He's wearing a covering made from papyrus. It's coated with a layer of plaster.

Narrator: The plaster was illustrated with human and god-like forms. And there were hieroglyphics from head to foot. A collar of glass beads hung around the Mummy's neck. There was a bead belt around his waist.

The men stripped off the papyrus. The doctor both spoke and wrote his observations.

Doctor Ponnonner: The flesh is in excellent condition. There is no odor. The color is reddish. And the skin is smooth and glossy. The teeth and hair look good. The eyes have been replaced with glass balls. The fingers and the nails are painted with gold.

Mr. Gliddon: The Mummy was embalmed.

From the smell, I'd say they used camphor and other gums.

Narrator: They all searched the body carefully. They were looking for openings through which guts had been removed. But there were none!

Doctor Ponnonner: I think I'll prepare my instruments. I'm going to dissect the Mummy.

John: It is past two o'clock, you know. Why don't we put off the internal exam?

Doctor Ponnonner: Okay, gentlemen. We'll meet tomorrow evening. Does that work for everyone?

John: Yes. Thank you, Ponnonner.

Mr. Gliddon: Fine with me.

Mr. Buckingham: Tomorrow it is.

Mr. Gliddon: Wait a moment. I have an idea. Why don't we try an experiment with the batteries? Just for sport.

Narrator: The men loved the idea. Mostly in jest, they set up a battery in the doctor's study. Then they cut back some of the Mummy's skin. And they attached the wires to his skull.

Nothing happened. They all laughed. But suddenly, John started waving his arms. And he shouted.

John: The Mummy's eyes! Look! The eyelids are fluttering!

Narrator: The men were very frightened. But they did calm down. Eventually.

Act III

Narrator: The men decided to do more tests. So they readjusted the battery. Then they exposed a toe muscle and attached the wire.

With a sudden jerk, the Mummy drew up his right knee. He kicked Doctor Ponnonner hard! The doctor shot through a window and fell to the street below.

John: Ponnonner! Come on, men. Let's go help him.

Doctor Ponnonner: No need, fellows. I'm back. I got up and ran right back upstairs. Let's try it again.

Narrator: The doctor did just that. First, the Mummy's eyes blinked quickly for several minutes. Second, the Mummy sneezed. Third, it sat up. Fourth, it shook its fist at Doctor

Ponnonner. And fifth, it spoke to Gliddon and Buckingham in Egyptian.

The Mummy: Gentlemen! I am shocked at your behavior. Doctor Ponnonner is a fool. He knows no better. So I pity him.

But you, Mr. Gliddon! And Buckingham! You've lived in Egypt. You speak Egyptian as well as your own language. You have always been regarded as a friend to the mummies. I expected more of you!

What am I to think? You permit Tom, Dick, and Harry to strip me of my clothes. It's cold in here!

Narrator: Oddly, none of the men acted as though anything unusual had happened. The Mummy sneered at them.

The Mummy: Why don't you speak, Mr. Buckingham? Didn't you hear what I said?

Narrator: Mr. Buckingham shuffled nervously from foot to foot. But he didn't answer. So the Egyptian turned to Mr. Gliddon. He demanded to know what was going on. Mr. Gliddon explained in Egyptian.

The rest of the conversations involving the Mummy were carried out in Egyptian. Gliddon and Buckingham interpreted for the rest of the men.

Mr. Gliddon: I assure you that our motives were pure. Surely you can understand the scientific benefits of studying mummies. But we do apologize for any trouble we have caused you. Right, gentlemen?

Mr. Buckingham: Yes!

John: Most certainly!

Doctor Ponnonner: Without a doubt!

The Mummy: Very well. I accept your apologies.

Narrator: The men rushed to the Mummy's side. Then they hurriedly stitched up the Mummy's forehead. They bandaged his foot. They applied some black plaster to his nose. And the doctor fetched some clothes for him to wear. The Egyptian was about half the doctor's size. So it was no small task to dress him.

Mr. Gliddon: Come sit by the fire, good sir.

The Mummy: Thank you. That would feel good.

Doctor Ponnonner: I'll ring the servants for some refreshments.

Narrator: The talk soon turned lively. The men were so very curious.

Mr. Buckingham: Tell me something. Isn't it high time you were dead?

The Mummy: Why, no! I am little more than 700 years old. My father lived to be 1,000.

Narrator: A brisk series of questions and calculations followed. It became clear that the Mummy's age had been misjudged. It had been at least 5,050 years since he had been placed in his tomb.

Doctor Ponnonner: You died and were buried in Egypt 5,000 years ago. So how is it that you are here today—alive and looking so well?

The Mummy: Ah, but I was not dead. I had fallen into a coma. And my friends decided that I was either dead or should be. So they embalmed me at once. I guess that you know about our embalming process?

Doctor Ponnonner: Not altogether.

The Mummy: What a sad state of ignorance you live in! Briefly, if the person was dead when he was embalmed, then he is dead now. But if he was alive, he is alive today. My situation was an accident. But some people were embalmed alive on purpose.

John: But why?

The Mummy: Well, a man's life lasted about 800 years. In my time, few men died before the age of 600. And few lived longer than 1,000 years.

Mr. Buckingham: Go on.

The Mummy: The embalming process was discovered. And our philosophers had an idea. They wanted to divide this natural life term into parts.

Narrator: The Mummy looked up. He was met with puzzled stares.

The Mummy: Let me explain the life parts. A man might live for 200 years. He would get embalmed and rest for 1,000 years. Then he would be revived and live for 500 years. And so on. We knew that we could learn so much. The field of science could advance. And history would become clearer.

Mr. Gliddon: Forgive me, sir. But I'm afraid you've lost me.

John: Me too.

The Mummy: Consider this, then. A historian, having lived to be 500, would write a book. Then he would get embalmed. He would leave instructions to be revived in 600 years. At this time, he would no doubt find different opinions about the work he'd left behind. He would thus rewrite it. So the current generation of people could understand it.

Doctor Ponnonner: Brilliant! Tell us more!

The Mummy: The historian would find out what else the moderns were saying about his time. He would be able to correct whatever misinformation there was. This process has kept Egyptian history alive. And accurate!

John: Tell us about astrology!

Mr. Buckingham: What are your thoughts on democracy?

Mr. Gliddon: What about your religious traditions?

Narrator: The Mummy addressed each issue in great detail. It was clear to the party that modern man was no match for the ancient Egyptians.

At one point, Dr. Ponnonner became excited. He had been feeling jealous. And he thought he'd found the perfect example of modern man's superiority.

Doctor Ponnonner: But look at our architecture! The Bowling Green Fountain in New York! Or the Capitol at Washington, D.C.!

Why, the Capitol's entrance has 420 columns. The columns are five feet in diameter and ten feet apart.

The Mummy: Hmmm. I wish I could remember exactly. But there was a small palace I knew in Carnac. It had 144 columns. They were 37 feet around. And 25 feet apart.

To get there from the Nile, one had to travel a two-mile avenue. It had sphinxes, statues, and pillars—20, 60, and 100 feet tall!

Narrator: The Mummy paused. But for just a moment. He had much more to say on the matter.

The Mummy: Now the palace itself was two miles long. And I think it was seven miles in circuit. Its walls were painted—inside and out.

I'd say that 200 of your Capitols could have been squeezed into that palace. With a little effort, of course!

You are right about one thing, Doctor Ponnonner. I cannot ignore it. The Fountain at the Bowling Green is magnificent. Superior. Nothing like it has ever been seen in Egypt— or anywhere else!

Narrator: The doctor was shattered. He shook his head. Then a light seemed to go on in his mind.

Doctor Ponnonner: Tell me, sir. Wouldn't the people of Egypt be impressed by the cleverness of modern dress?

Narrator: The Egyptian glanced at the pantaloons the doctor had given him. Then he examined the end of one of his coat-tails. Slowly, his mouth formed a grin from ear to ear.

The Mummy: Indeed!

Doctor Ponnonner: May I ask one more thing—upon your honor as a gentleman?

The Mummy: Of course.

Doctor Ponnonner: Have the Egyptians heard of, at any time, the manufacture of Ponnonner's lozenges? Or Brandreth's pills?

Narrator: The Egyptian hung his head. He blushed. He had no answer! And he was deeply ashamed. Clearly, the doctor had finally bested the Mummy.

John could not bear to watch it. So he grabbed his hat, bowed stiffly, and left the scene.

Act IV

Narrator: It was past four o'clock in the morning when John got home. He went to bed immediately. His wife yelled at him for disturbing her sleep.

At seven o'clock, John got up again. His mind was racing.

John's Wife: What are you doing now? You're getting dressed? Are you leaving again?

John: Yes. I'm leaving. And I won't be back. Not while you're alive, anyway.

John's Wife: What kind of nonsense is that? Have you gone mad?

John: On the contrary! I've seen the light! I am sick of this life. And I am sick of the 19th century. Maybe I'll return in 2045. Just to see who's president.

John's Wife: You're babbling! I don't understand this foolishness.

John: You don't have to! Good-bye!